angus, thongs and perfect snogging

TOP GOSSIP!

www.georgianicolson.com

HarperCollins *Children's Books*

TOP GOSSIP!

Georgia Nicolson's not going mental, but her life is

angus, thongs and perfect snogging

LATE

35

DIR: GURINDER CHADHA

Angus, Thongs an

SEPT '0

First published in Great Britain in 2008 by HarperCollins Children's Books,
a division of HarperCollins Publishers Ltd.,
77 - 85 Fulham Palace Road, Hammersmith, London, W6 8JB

The HarperCollins website address is: www.harpercollinschildrensbooks.co.uk

Find out more about Georgia at: www.georgianicolson.com

1 3 5 7 9 10 8 6 4 2

ISBN13: 978-0-00-728087-2
ISBN: 0-00-728087-4

Have you seen the most marvy, megafab
and officially hottest film of 2008...
Angus, Thongs and Perfect Snogging,
starring Georgia and her besties yet?
Well what are you waiting for?!

Here's all the top gossip from Georgia's big
screen debut: character profiles, hot pics,
cool party ideas, puzzles and quizzes, and lots of
tres groovy things to amuse you, not to
mention more than a few shots of the
Stiff Dylans...

Fabbity-fab!

X

Contents

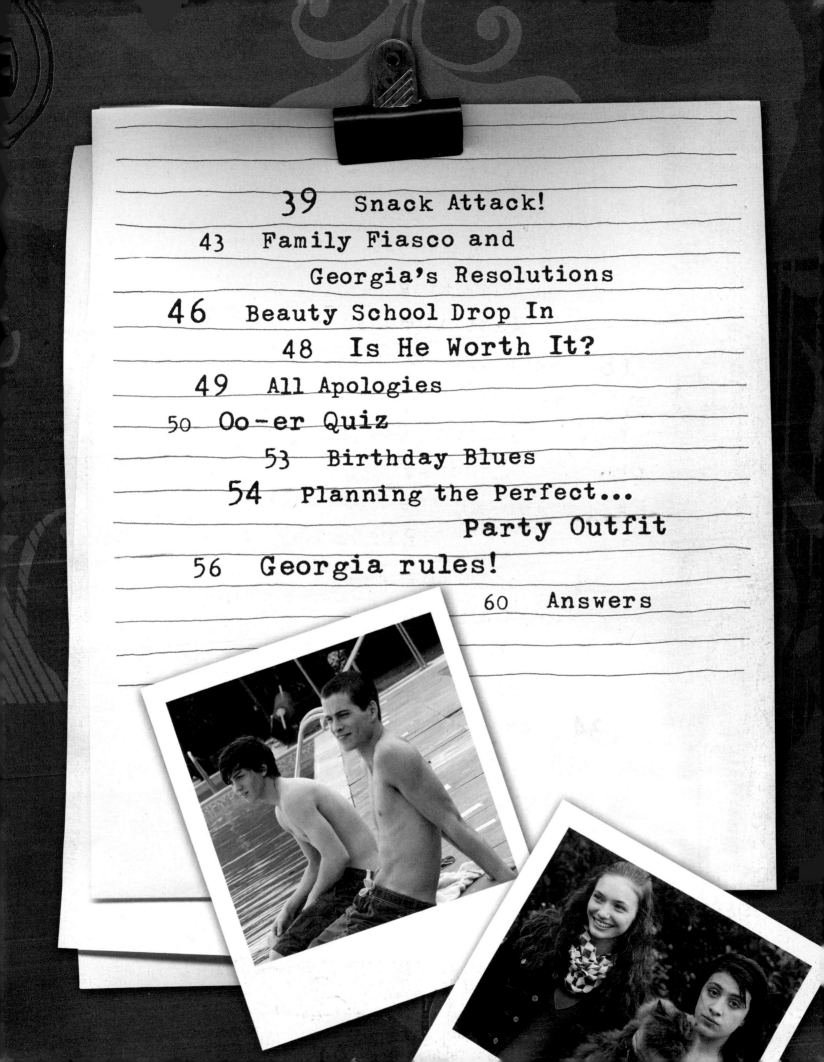

Name: Georgia Nicolson

Age: 14 (nearly 15!)

Birthday: Oh sooooo soon...

Star Sign: Erm, I'll get back to you on that

Address: Madland, Loon Street, Eastbourne, UK

Phone Number: As if my dad has let me get a mobile... Sad but true.

School: Ridgley

Best Friends: The Ace Gang – Jas, Ellen and Rosie

Favourite Food: Jammie dodgers, pop tarts

Favourite Film: Whatever George Clooney is in (he may be ancient but he's still a fittie)

Favourite Website: Youtube

Favourite Book: Men are from Mars, Women are from Venus (otherwise known as The Boy Bible)

Favourite Mag: Sugar

Favourite Song: Ultraviolet by Stiff Dylans

Favourite Band: Do you have to ask? Stiff Dylans of course!

Best Outfit: Boots, mini skirt and sparkly top (accessorised with mum's handbag if I can borrow it without her noticing)

Favourite Animal: Angus – my half mad Scottish wildcat

Favourite Munchies at a sleepover: Jas' midget gems

Favourite Luuurve God: Robbie

8

Georgia Nicolson

...founder of the Ace Gang
and *Sex Kitty* of the first order.

Luuurves her family and
BESTIES even if they drive her
a bit crazy.

Not so sure that her dad's new job offer in
New Zealand is the best thing for the Nicolsons
(although it will be easier to get a DJ for her
upcoming birthday party if there's only one
parent around to convince).

On the verge of *womanhood*, bravely
venturing into the land of snogging and
beset by the worries of *boys*,

basoomas,

bust ups and best friend betrayals... how will she cope
with all that being nearly fifteen throws at her?

MOST LIKELY TO SAY:
I see a snog at the end of the tunnel!

LEAST LIKELY TO SAY: *Lindsay's my bestie.*

The Six Things Very Wrong With my Life

1) My mum and dad hate me doing what I
want, probably cause they know their lives are
practically over and mine's just starting.

2) 'The olds' won't let me get a mobile, a lock on my
door, a nose job, or a party I want cause they can't
face the fact I'm a woman now.

3) My little sister thinks she's a cat and peed
somewhere in my room. Poor Angus will need even more
therapy than me.

4) I am very ugly and need to go into an ugly home.

5) I will never get a boyfriend because everyone will
see me as Olive Girl after my disastrous appearance at
the fancy dress party (how come everyone else changed
their minds about going as canapés?)

6) I only have one eyebrow...after a mishap with Dad's
razor. Eek!

Jas

Key member of the **Ace Gang**
and number **one** bestie of Georgia.

Prepared to risk life and limb for her in
operation **Angus Advantage**.

Always on hand with semi-useless advice
and one half of the brains behind the
Snogging Scale - the Ten Stages of Snogging
(the turnip half, naturally).

Smitten with hottie **Tom** on first sight
and happy to devote herself to a lifetime
of **vegetables** for him.

MOST LIKELY TO SAY:
What does he mean, see you later?

LEAST LIKELY TO SAY:
Maths is better than boys.

Ellen

The 'bit innocent' one,
Ellen's the late adopter when it comes
to **boys** but she knows a **hottie**
when she sees one!

MOST LIKELY TO SAY:
Friends are forever, boys come and go.

LEAST LIKELY TO SAY:
Why is three-timing boys so complicated?

Rosie

The most experienced
girl in the Ace Gang,

having got herself a boyfriend in the
form of Swedish exchange student, Sven,

(who thinks he's Scandinavia's answer to 50 Cent).

Keen on snogging with all the trimmings
and the **looniest** of the bunch.

Maybe because she's from Wales.

MOST LIKELY TO SAY:
The snogging's wicked!

LEAST LIKELY TO SAY:
I think I'll become a nun.

Georgia's besties:
Jas, Rosie, Ellen
also known as
the Ace Gang
(including Georgia
of course!)

The Ace Gang go to the most deeply
unfab school, **Ridgley**, along
with some really cringe-making people...

Nauseating Pamela Green
- the girl who breeds **hamsters**. Enough said.

The Bummer Twins
- chain-smoking school **bullies**.

Dave the Laugh
- erm, lighting your **farts** is funny?

Lindsay 'Slag' Marling
- queen of mean and Georgia's arch **rival**.

Thankfully Georgia's mates make up for everyone else!

When the Ace Gang see the fittest boys EVER at school...

they know its boy-stalking time!

Georgia and Jas spot that they work at the new organic shop

So after a quick check for minty fresh breath

they drop by... turns out Tom and Robbie are twins!

Jas likes Tom...

and Georgia likes Robbie, who is in a cool band called Stiff Dylans.

But then Georgia sees Robbie with his arm around Slaggy Lindsay:

she might have lost him before she even got him.

So the Ace Gang decide to find out what makes Lindsay so attractive and mature...

and discover her hidden secrets — a THONG from Vulgaria AND fake boobs!!

To make sure she's up to speed,

Georgia takes a lesson in snogging from geeky Peter Dyer...

its a trip to saliva city (Ew)...

with unwanted results.

13

STIFF DYLANS

PLUS SUPPORT AND SPECIAL GUESTS!
BRIGHTON @ SHELL SHOCK
DOORS 7PM, £5 ON THE DOOR

It's the hotties you've been waiting for...presenting the Stiff Dylans!

Robbie

Total Sex God and the best bass player ever!

Plays: bass guitar
Fave track: Ever Fallen in Love (With Someone You Shouldn't've) – Buzzcocks
Secret crush: You tell me!

James

Plays: guitar and vocals
Fave track: Creep – Radiohead
Secret crush: Robbie's mum!

Matt

Plays: bass guitar
Fave track: Big Fan – Stiff Dylans
Secret crush: She knows who she is...

Charlie

Plays: lead guitar
Fave track: Ultraviolet – Stiff Dylans
Secret crush: Miss Stamp!

Tom S

Plays: drums
Fave track: She Drives Me Crazy – Stiff Dylans
Secret crush: All our fans

Interview with the band

Q. So, Stiff Dylans how did you get together?
A. (Robbie) Well I've always been really into music so when I hooked up with the others there was no question - Stiff Dylans had to happen.

Q. What other bands do you rate?
A. Radiohead, Pink Floyd, Buzzcocks, Bloc Party, Foo Fighters

Q. What's your fave song in your set list?
A. Ultraviolet - it rocks!

Q. Who thought of the band name?
A. (all in unison) Me!

Q. What's the best thing about being in a band?
A. We love performing to a crowd, its so great seeing everyone singing along and going crazy. And the girls love it!

Q. What's the worst?
A. Having to lug the kit around - the amps weigh a ton.

Q. Where do you get your song writing inspiration?
A. (Robbie) I usually go down to the beach and just think about stuff that's been going on and start from there.

Q. What are your songs about?
A. Well, life, you know, the universe and how reality TV is brainwashing everyone - that kinda thing.

Q. What are your pet hates?
A. Boredom, queuing, fights and burgers (we're vegetarians).

Q. Any last words for your fans?
A. We luuurve you all - so keep it Stiff!

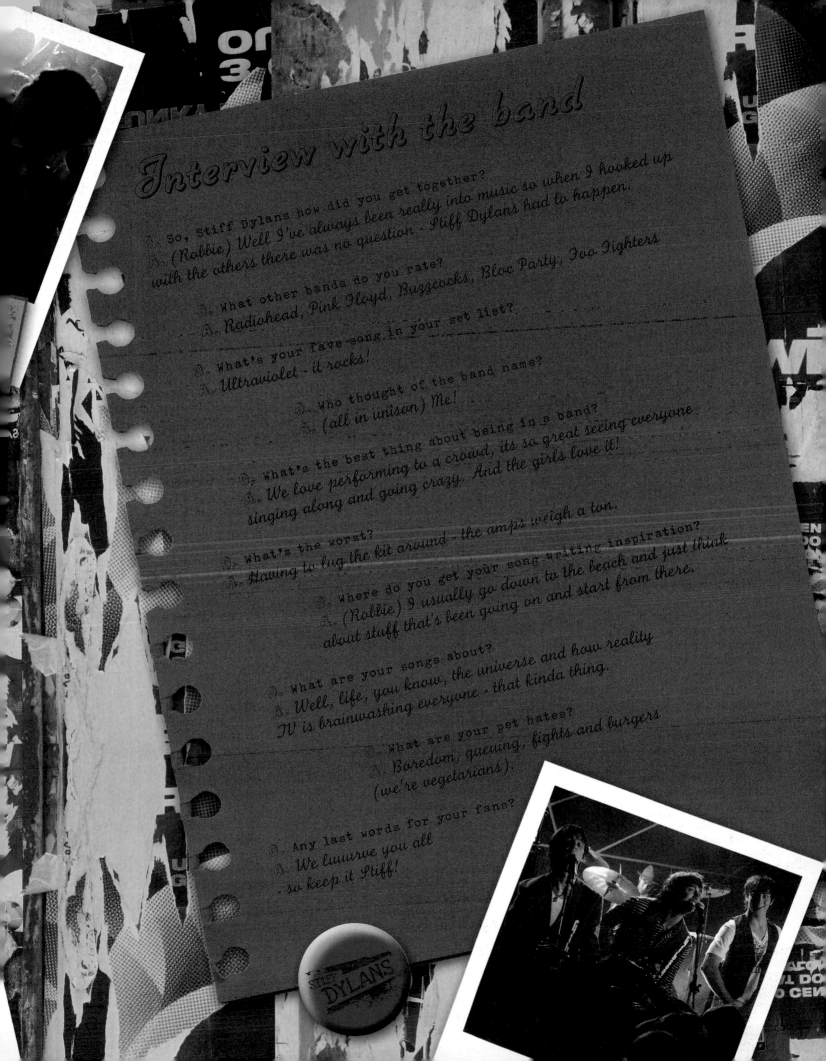

Ultraviolet

by Stiff Dylans

He is a wave and he's breaking
He's a problem to solve
And in that circle he's making
I will always revolve
And on his sight
These eyes depend
Invisible and indivisible

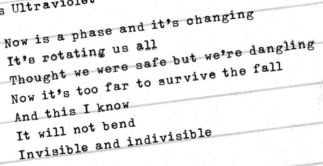

That fire you ignited
Good bad and undecided
Burned when I stand beside it
Your light is Ultraviolet
Visions so insane
They travel unravelling through my brain
Cold when I am denied it
Your light is Ultraviolet

Now is a phase and it's changing
It's rotating us all
Thought we were safe but we're dangling
Now it's too far to survive the fall
And this I know
It will not bend
Invisible and indivisible

That fire you ignited
Good bad and undecided
Burned when I stand beside it
Your light is Ultraviolet
Visions so insane
They travel unravelling through my brain
Cold when I am denied it
Your light is Ultraviolet

That fire you ignited
Good bad and undecided
Burned when I stand beside it
Your light is Ultraviolet
Visions so insane
They travel unravelling through my brain
Cold nearly froze outside it
Your light is Ultraviolet

ULTRAVIOLET
Written by Scott Cutler and Ann Preven
©2002 Stage Three Songs/Scott Cutler Music (ASCAP) and Music of Stage Three/Weetie Pie Music (BMI)
Administered by Stage Three Music (U.S) Inc. All Rights Reserved. Used by permission. Int'l Copyright Secured

Meet The Loon Family

The Nicolson family, affectionately nicknamed the **Loon** Family by Georgia. She luuurves them deep down but the elderly snoggers (her parents) and her cheeky little sister sometimes drive her round the bend.

Connie

Georgia's mum, the owner of coveted goods such as *designer* handbags and clothes that are too young for her (that she should naturally donate to her daughter who is clearly on the verge of *womanhood*).

She also has books of eternal wisdom when it comes to boys such as *How to Make Any Twit Fall in Love with You* and *Men Are From Mars, Women Are From Venus.*

Strange that she ended up with Georgia's dad, but that is the mystery of luuurve. Although she seems quite keen on *hot* builders too.

MOST LIKELY TO SAY:
Georgia, I need you to babysit Libby tonight.

LEAST LIKELY TO SAY:
I think I'll just stay in, Corrie's on.

Bob

Georgia's dad, a.k.a. The Portly One. Blessed with the largest nose in the world which Georgia has unfortunately inherited.

A keen geologist who will go to the other side of the world to investigate geo-magnetics i.e. boring rocks, instead of being a proper dad like Jas's (who protects his family home from potential home-wreckers who happen to be cute builders called Jem).

MOST LIKELY TO SAY:
How many times have I told you not to run up the phone bill?

LEAST LIKELY TO SAY:
Of course you can have a mobile, Georgia, you deserve it.

Libby

Georgia's half-mad little sister seems convinced she is part human, part cat.

She and Angus spend plenty of time together, playing favourite games such as hiding in the fridge, using Georgia's make-up... and number one favourite, dressing up. So if Angus appears in drag, Libby is sure to be at the bottom of it.

MOST LIKELY TO SAY
(IN FRONT OF A CUTE BOY):
Georgia did a big poo!

LEAST LIKELY TO SAY:
Nothing and smile sweetly like her kindy classmates.

19

Angus

King of the Jungle,
Lord of the Scottish Wildcats

...and pet of Georgia.

Fearless stalker of poodles, small dogs or any animal foolish enough to go near him,

yet strangely compliant when Libby decides he wants to dress up as a cowboy or wear lipstick.

Will eat anything (including knickers) and is often to be found in the fridge or savaging Bob's sock drawer.

Grandad

makes his false teeth tap dance. In public. Enough said.

The Angus Advantage

Couldn't wait to meet Robbie and Tom? Neither could Georgia and Jas, but unfortunately Lindsay got there first...

So Georgia comes up with a plan - the Angus Advantage!

Georgia leaves Angus with Jas in the park...

Then she asks Robbie to put up a 'lost cat flyer' in the shop...

Robbie loves cats too,

so how could he resist helping Georgia when it seems that hers is 'lost'...

Robbie and Georgia go to the beach 'looking for Angus'...

... and Georgia impresses Robbie with her mean air guitar moves.

Meanwhile Jas is having trouble keeping hold of the mad cat...

and when it sees a poodle, Tom thankfully comes to the rescue.

Robbie and Georgia finally get to the park

and it looks like the plan is working!

Robbie happily hands Angus back to Georgia

and then Tom asks out Jas.

Fabbity fab!

All About Georgia Quiz

1. What is the name of Georgia's little sis?

   a. Libby
   b. Katie
   b. Lily

2. Which school does Georgia go to?

   a. Ridgley
   b. Bridgewater
   c. Ridgeway

3. Where does Georgia's dad go to work?

   a. America
   b. Australia
   c. New Zealand

4. What does Jas have that Georgia wants?

   a. Hair extensions
   b. An ipod
   c. A mobile phone

5. What is the nickname of Georgia's headmistress?

   a. Fattie
   b. Slim
   c. Skinny

6. What is the name of Georgia's arch enemy?

   a. Lindsay Marling
   b. Pamela Green
   c. Jas

7. Where does Georgia's cat come from?

   a. The Scottish Highlands
   b. The West Country
   c. The South Coast

8. Who is Georgia's dream date?

   a. Tom
   b. Jem
   c. Robbie

9. What does Georgia go to a party dressed as?

    a. Cocktail sausage
    b. Stuffed olive
    c. Cheese straw

10. Who teaches Georgia the art of snogging?

    a. Peter Dyer
    b. Dave the Laugh
    c. Sven

11. Name the Ace Gang...

    a. Jas, Rosie, Ellen and Georgia
    b. Jas, Pamela, Georgia and Ellen
    c. Yasmin, Rosie, Naomi and Georgia

12. What does Georgia get 4 out of 10 for?

    a. Her eyes
    b. Her nose
    c. Her personality

13. Who gives Georgia that score?

    a. Jas
    b. Libby
    c. Rosie

14. What is the name of Georgia's mun?

    a. Sally
    b. Connie
    c. Lucy

15. What is the name of Georgia's dad?

    a. Jeff
    b. Paul
    c. Bob

16. What does Georgia call New Zealand?

    a. Wombat-a-go-go-land
    b. Over there
    c. Kiwi-land

17. Where do Georgia and her family go out to dinner?

    a. Pizzeria
    b. Mexican restaurant
    c. Burger bar

Answers on page 60-61

With Dad safely packed
off to Kiwi-land,

Georgia begins her party
planning in earnest

but soon finds out she's in
competition with arch rival
Lindsay to host the best bash...

and Jas is choosing Tom
over the Ace Gang and thongs
instead of knickers.

At hockey, Lindsay
warns Georgia to stay
away from Robbie

and shows her mean streak...

shoving Georgia to
the ground.

Later the Ace Gang see
Robbie turning away from
an attempted snog with her

— is there hope for
Georgia yet?

Planning the Perfect Party

Birthday parties need serious **planning**,
so follow the steps below to host a party
you'll **never** forget. Remember to
check everything is ok with your folks first.
You don't want them ruining
the fun on the night – Eek!

Super Sophis Soiree

This party works best as a small gathering of your
closest friends so don't invite the whole world. Keep
your guest list under 15.

- Find a **venue** – you could hold the party in your living
room or a local restaurant.

- Work out your **decoration** theme – for a très sophis feel,
why not find some arty posters and use as a backdrop for
the *soirée*? Serve all your drinks in *cocktail* glasses for
that special *je ne sais quoi*.

- Plan a cool menu with mini hot dogs, bite-size
pizzas and chocolate mousse for desert.

- Make your own *fabbity-fab* juice cocktails. There are some
marvy ideas for food and drinks on pages 39-42.

- Design your invite to look really glam, perhaps just in
black and white with a touch of sparkle.

- Make sure everyone knows there is a dress code. All your
guests need to come in their FABBIEST outfits.

- Choose *music* to play at the party before your guests turn
up. Either make mix CDs or line up a playlist on your MP3
player so there's no chance of someone putting on your dad's
folk music by mistake. Eek! There are dozens of cool bands
like the STIFF DYLANS around – if you can't think of any look
them up online or ask your friends to bring their faves.

- If you want to be super sophis, why not ask your pals
to speak in *French* for the evening – *au contraire* and
ooh la la!

swanky Sleepover Party

There aren't many rules for planning the perfect sleepover party but always remember these top five tips:

- Check with your parents
- Confirm the date with everyone well in advance
- Make sure everyone knows what they need to bring
- Make sure everyone has a way to get home the next day
- Make sure you clean up afterwards!

List of everything you need to take to a sleepover

Sleeping bag and pillow
PJs
Slippers if it's cold
Toothbrush
Clothes and underwear for the next day
Snacks (lots of them)

List of everything you need to throw a sleepover

A big empty room
Lots of spare quilts and pillows in case your friends forget theirs or get chilly
Lots of plastic cups
Kitchen towel to clean up any spillages
Paper plates
Make-up and remover
Nail varnish
Nail varnish remover pads
TV/DVD player
CD player
Drinks and snacks

Themed Sleepovers

Themed sleepovers are fabbity fab so let your *imagination* run wild and free...

Before you settle down for the sleepover party, why not head to the nearest outdoor ice rink, go to the cinema or indulge in some girlie SHOPPING!

Ask your friends to bring their fave movies (as long as that doesn't mean The Wizard of Oz. Again.) Don't forget the popcorn.

Try some of the Ace Gang recipes – the mini pizzas are really easy and *yummy*.

Treat yourselves to *spa* treatments – give all of your friends a manicure and pedicure, then do mini makeovers on each other.

Major Boy Fiasco

Georgia continues her campaign to be more sophis and Robbie-entrancing...

but at Kirstie Walsh's party there's a major boy fiasco when Peter Dyer tries his luck again...

and knocks Georgia into a flower bed in a snogging attempt revealing her knickers to everyone

... including Robbie and Lindsay! Deeply unfab.

Meanwhile, Georgia's mum and Jem the builder are getting on rather too well —

she's even taking him to her salsa class...

and it looks like Dad's staying in Kiwi-land forever...

Ace Gang Quiz

1. Where is Rosie's boyfriend from?

a. Lapland
b. France
c. Sweden

2. Who does Jas fancy?

a. Sven
b. Dave the Laugh
c. Tom

3. What is a nervy b?

a. A jumpy insect
b. A scared bunny
c. An attack of the nerves

4. What is the name of Rosie's boyfriend?

a. Stan
b. Sven
c. Steffan

5. What is Robbie's band called?

a. Straight Denims
b. Strong Diamonds
c. Stiff Dylans

6. What does Dave the Laugh want to be when he leaves school?

a. Stand-up comedian
b. Talk show host
c. Circus performer

7. What is Robbie's part-time job?

a. Working at the supermarket
b. Lifeguard
c. Helping out at his mum's organic shop

8. Where does Robbie and Tom's dad live?

a. Eastbourne
b. London
c. New York

9. What animal does Nauseating Pamela Green breed?

a. Voles
b. Stick insects
c. Hamsters

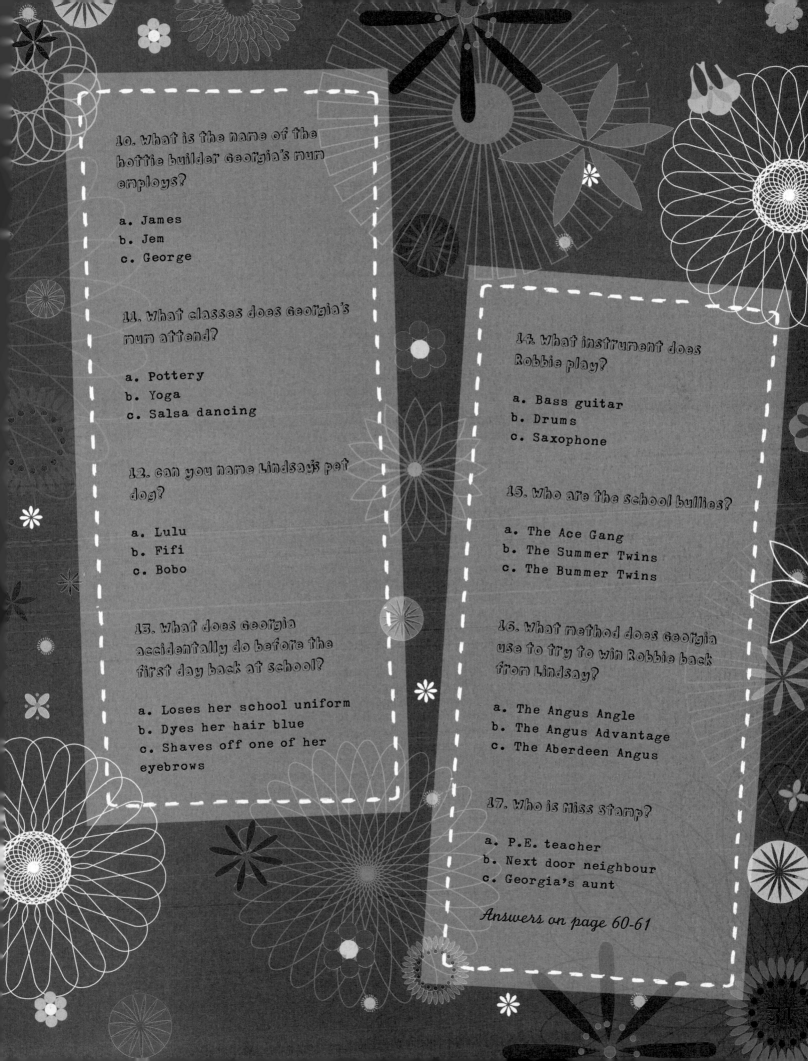

10. What is the name of the hottie builder Georgia's mum employs?

a. James
b. Jem
c. George

11. What classes does Georgia's mum attend?

a. Pottery
b. Yoga
c. Salsa dancing

12. Can you name Lindsay's pet dog?

a. Lulu
b. Fifi
c. Bobo

13. What does Georgia accidentally do before the first day back at school?

a. Loses her school uniform
b. Dyes her hair blue
c. Shaves off one of her eyebrows

14. What instrument does Robbie play?

a. Bass guitar
b. Drums
c. Saxophone

15. Who are the school bullies?

a. The Ace Gang
b. The Summer Twins
c. The Bummer Twins

16. What method does Georgia use to try to win Robbie back from Lindsay?

a. The Angus Angle
b. The Angus Advantage
c. The Aberdeen Angus

17. Who is Miss Stamp?

a. P.E. teacher
b. Next door neighbour
c. Georgia's aunt

Answers on page 60-61

Boy bananas and Elastic Band Theory

Jas (via Tom) lets Robbie know Georgia's accidental knicker-flashing was not boyfriend related...

...and Operation Swimming Pool takes place!

Robbie, Jas and Tom are going swimming

so Georgia jumps at the chance to see Robbie and takes Libby along to the pool...

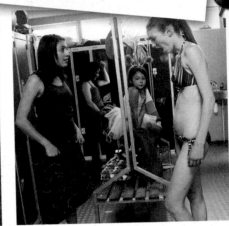

but a pre-swim fake tan disaster needs covering up.

Things are going swimmingly...

until Georgia forgets that her legs look like two giant cheesy puffs!

Thankfully Robbie finds this hilarious and can't resist diving in for a Perfect snog! Yes! He promises to call...

It's no surprise that Lindsay changes the date of her party to directly clash with Georgia's (after seeing Jas' invitation), but when Robbie doesn't call or invite Georgia to his gig on Saturday night

thankfully her mum is on hand with the Boy Bible – Men Are From Mars, Women Are From Venus.

Georgia learns the fine art of...

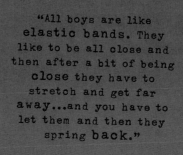

"All boys are like elastic bands. They like to be all close and then after a bit of being close they have to stretch and get far away...and you have to let them and then they spring back."

Elastic Band Theory.

A PLAN OF MATURIOSITY AND GLACIOSITY

STEP 1. Georgia must ask Robbie's mate Dave the Laugh to the gig.

This is to prove to Robbie that she is sophisticated and grown-up - the Maturiosity bit.

STEP 2. Georgia must be distant and alluring and play hard to get - the ice-cool Glaciosity bit.

STEP 3. Then Robbie will come springing back into Georgia's arms and chuck Lindsay.

Georgia's plan sort of works

and Robbie's clearly ruffled by the attention she's paying Dave...

but she gets more than she bargained for when Dave tries to snog her good night.

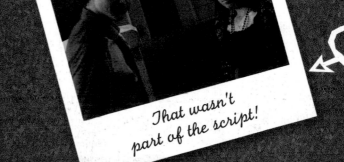

That wasn't part of the script!

33

Ace Gang Wordsearch

Can you find all the words in this
giant wordsearch? Everything is
related to Georgia and pals.

Y	P	D	X	U	F	M	S	E	Y	B	B	I	L	A	P	H	Y	B	O	B	P	H	N	B
A	S	M	Y	R	S	L	S	N	V	F	N	D	T	Y	Z	E	Y	A	B	A	Q	O	P	S
W	N	E	O	N	T	C	I	E	R	T	A	E	H	T	L	A	O	G	R	F	M	L	L	N
S	G	L	E	L	K	B	N	Z	I	M	A	S	P	H	D	N	Z	T	T	A	L	L	D	O
N	D	N	U	V	S	K	B	J	N	E	A	P	S	H	H	W	Y	L	N	G	U	Y	Z	G
A	S	F	I	N	S	E	R	E	L	A	S	A	T	G	E	L	E	S	R	E	Y	W	D	G
L	Y	P	U	P	A	M	C	A	N	S	O	R	Q	P	S	Y	M	I	R	M	L	O	U	I
Y	T	S	Y	C	J	O	B	U	P	T	I	R	S	T	K	N	K	P	G	W	W	O	A	N
D	Z	C	H	V	N	O	N	A	R	B	A	K	O	S	N	F	Q	K	U	O	Y	D	E	G
F	E	R	O	X	G	L	H	A	W	O	X	M	U	S	U	A	E	U	H	A	S	Y	L	S
F	K	S	R	K	I	D	U	S	F	U	O	O	H	P	I	C	F	V	F	B	P	X	L	C
I	S	V	T	A	R	Q	C	L	E	R	B	H	A	F	C	E	K	B	S	X	T	I	E	A
T	K	E	I	B	B	O	R	X	U	N	B	O	F	C	Z	G	O	A	K	B	J	M	N	L
S	E	H	W	S	U	B	I	I	S	E	G	S	S	D	T	A	G	N	S	L	F	H	G	E
J	C	F	E	W	E	R	D	V	H	W	O	D	J	J	M	N	H	A	M	K	F	O	B	H
Y	D	M	P	R	R	E	G	N	C	Y	O	R	X	L	U	G	R	A	K	C	I	U	B	M
H	I	I	T	S	D	B	L	N	R	G	T	K	I	N	N	Y	Y	F	D	U	M	X	K	B
T	O	Y	R	X	W	R	E	O	E	R	O	V	A	N	M	Y	Z	G	D	N	Q	H	E	J
V	Z	U	Q	E	T	B	Y	V	Z	K	H	G	H	F	V	H	O	S	U	G	N	A	G	H
H	V	A	L	F	C	K	R	T	T	L	N	A	S	N	Z	B	F	L	X	M	N	B	R	Q
Z	F	T	X	Y	E	U	M	O	D	U	L	M	D	R	Y	M	A	B	E	F	K	H	B	I
U	A	B	U	T	U	U	O	P	N	V	N	I	J	L	J	A	C	Y	W	U	C	K	F	O
N	F	A	T	U	Y	J	U	R	H	M	G	E	O	R	G	I	A	F	U	H	Z	L	Z	J
F	U	E	L	T	E	U	S	F	Y	K	M	P	F	N	O	I	A	E	Q	E	N	X	X	A
F	S	I	L	H	H	X	Q	E	H	A	F	A	B	B	I	T	Y	F	A	B	C	T	Y	Q

GEORGIA   JAS ᶦᶜˢ   ROSIE   ELLEN

ROBBIE   TOM   STIFF DYLANS   ACE GANG

EASTBOURNE   RIDGLEY   PARTY   FABBITY FAB

NUNGA NUNGAS   BIRTHDAY   SNOGGING SCALE

MEGAFAB   LUUURVE GODS   ANGUS   LIBBY

The
Ace Gang
Dance
Routine

As dance floor minxes of the highest order,
the Ace Gang have invented some
megafab dance routines.
Follow these instructions to strut
your stuff Ace Gang style:

Stamp stamp left,
stamp stamp right,
Big box, little box,
Big box, little box

Shimmy, shimmy forward
Shimmy, shimmy back
Big box, little box,
Big box, little box

Point to the left, point to the right
Fold arms, nod, fold arms, nod

Spin around
Big box, little box
High five!

Repeat
until
dizziness
takes
over...

Create a beautiful lasting **memento** of you and your *favourite pals* by following these simple steps.

1. Give each of your pals a piece of sticky tape slightly longer than their nose.

2. Attach the sticky tape to nose and forehead, starting at nostril end, gently lifting your 'snout' upwards.

3. Set a camera with a timer switch, arrange yourselves in a charming group shot...

4. Et voila!
A perfect pigture of you and your Ace Gang.

Everything goes from unfab to deeply unfab for Georgia:

Dave asks her about 'elastic band theory' and calls her a heartless upson cause he found out about her plans from Tom, who found out from so-called bestie, Jas...

Georgia confronts Jas on the netball court and soon insults are flying...

Georgia calls Jas a backstabber...

and Jas calls Georgia jealous and scheming...

so Georgia loses it...

and is sent to do litter duty
as punishment.

Then when things couldn't
get any worse,

Robbie breaks her heart by telling
her she's just a kid and that all
she thinks about is herself.

Sob.

Meanwhile, her mum's out
with the builder yet again...

Snack Attack

When Georgia's home alone
with nothing left in the fridge,
she relies on some handy
DIY recipes - enjoy!

Georgia's Groovy Mini Pizzas

Serves 2

2 bagels or white rolls sliced in half
Tomato puree
2 big handfuls of grated cheese
8 small slices of pepperoni or ham

1. Spread a tablespoon of tomato puree on to each of the bagel halves.
2. Top with a sprinkling of cheese, then a layer of pepperoni (or ham) and then another sprinkling of cheese.
3. Toast under the grill until the cheese begins to bubble and turn golden brown.

P.S. If you're a veggie, then swap the pepperoni for red or green peppers and sliced tomato.

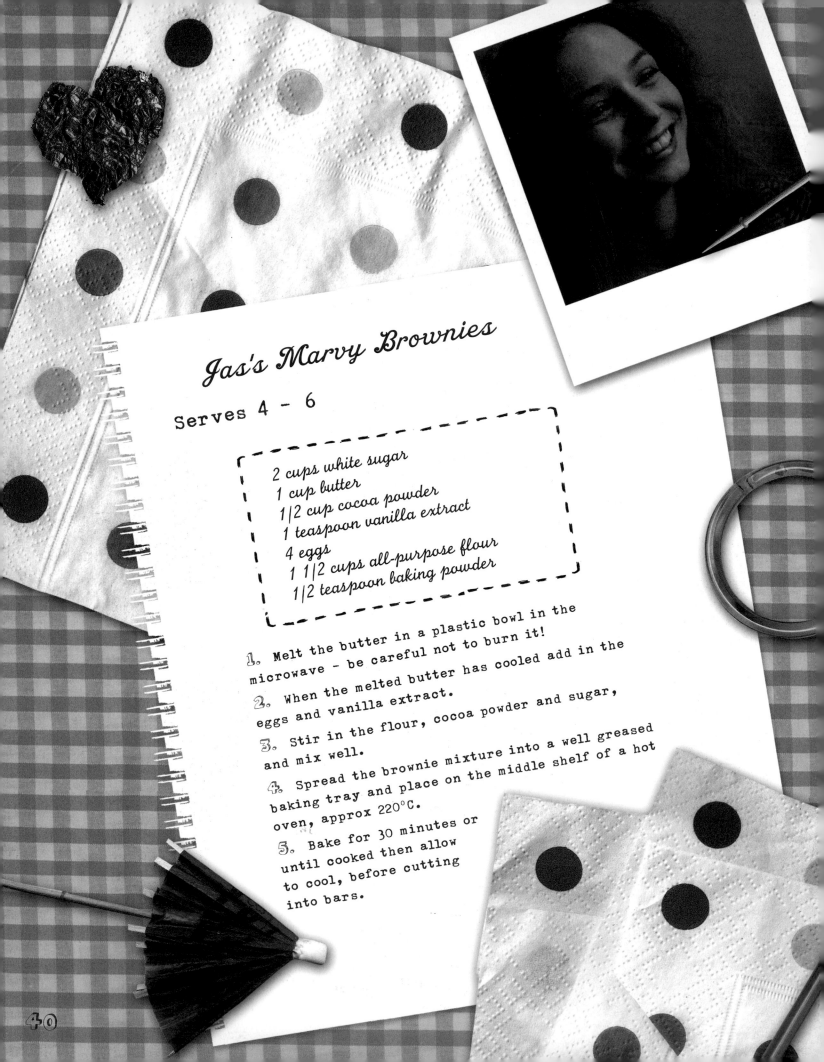

Jas's Marvy Brownies

Serves 4 - 6

2 cups white sugar
1 cup butter
1|2 cup cocoa powder
1 teaspoon vanilla extract
4 eggs
1 1|2 cups all-purpose flour
1|2 teaspoon baking powder

1. Melt the butter in a plastic bowl in the microwave – be careful not to burn it!

2. When the melted butter has cooled add in the eggs and vanilla extract.

3. Stir in the flour, cocoa powder and sugar, and mix well.

4. Spread the brownie mixture into a well greased baking tray and place on the middle shelf of a hot oven, approx 220°C.

5. Bake for 30 minutes or until cooked then allow to cool, before cutting into bars.

Ellen's Fabbity-fab Fizz

Serves 8

1 large tin pineapple juice
1 small tin mandarin segments
1 carton fresh orange juice
2 litres of low-sugar lemon and lime fizzy drink

1. Mix the orange juice and pineapple juice in a large freezer proof container.
2. Drain the mandarin segments and add them to the drink.
3. Add in the lemon and lime drink then place in the fridge.
4. Freeze for at least three hours and then serve frozen and slushy. The lemon and lime makes the drink fizz on your tongue!

Rosie's Super Sophis Smoothie

Serves 4

1 cup crushed pineapple
4 fresh apricots, diced
20 strawberries
2 bananas

1. Blitz the bananas and pineapple in a blender until they are smooth.
2. Add the apricots and 3/4 of the strawberries.
3. Pour the smoothie into tall glasses filled with ice.
4. Slice the remaining strawberries and drop them on top of the smoothies.

The Ace Gang's ICE COOL CRUSH

1 carton fresh orange juice
1 carton cranberry juice
A hand full of fresh mint to serve

1. Pour the orange juice into a small plastic bowl and the cranberry into another.

2. Place the bowls carefully in the freezer and leave for 3 hours until they are almost completely frozen.

3. Scoop out the ice and crush into crystals, then layer a scoop of orange on top of a scoop of cranberry until your glass is full.

4. Garnish with a spring of mint.

Family Fiasco

Convinced that her parents are on the verge of divorce, Georgia decides to gatecrash her mum's salsa dance class…

Georgia sneaks in to spy on the class…

and sees Jem…

and Connie dancing closer than close.

Georgia is mortified and runs to her dad's old office…

to try and ask for him to come home before her family break up.

And faces the fact that she may have to move to New Zealand after all.

43

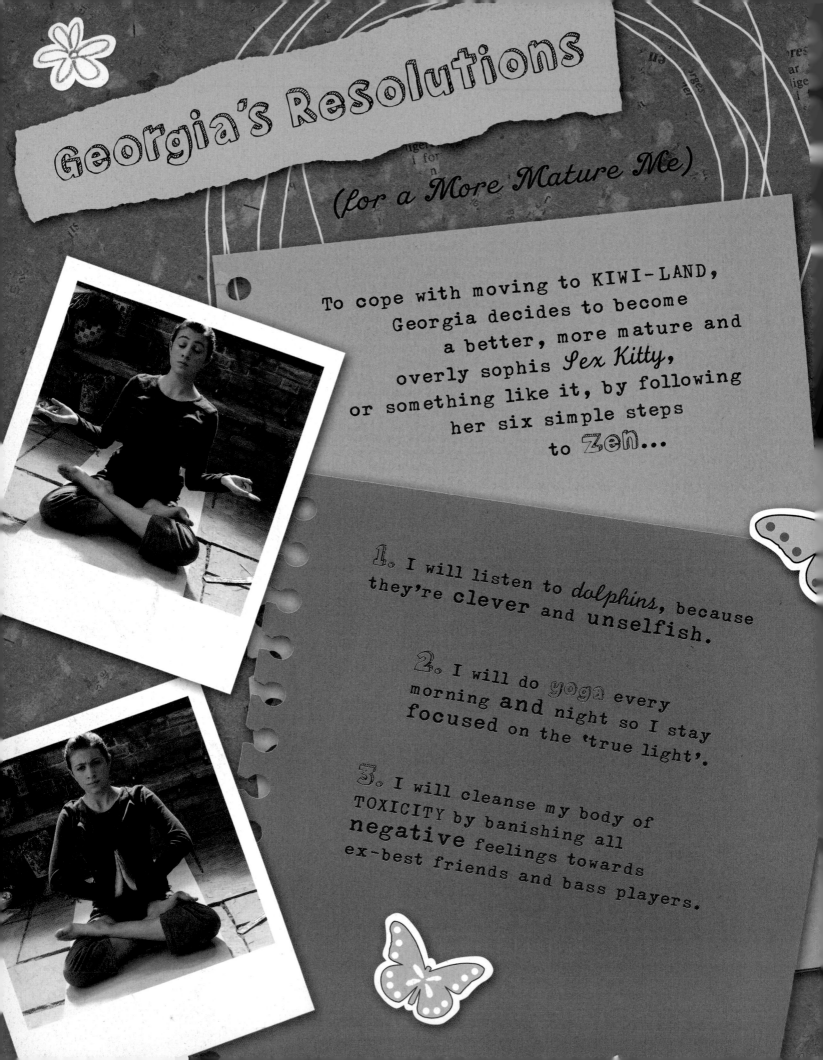

Georgia's Resolutions

(for a More Mature Me)

To cope with moving to KIWI-LAND, Georgia decides to become a better, more mature and overly sophis *Sex Kitty*, or something like it, by following her six simple steps to zen...

1. I will listen to *dolphins*, because they're **clever** and **unselfish**.

2. I will do *yoga* every morning **and** night so I stay focused on the 'true light'.

3. I will cleanse my body of TOXICITY by banishing all **negative** feelings towards ex-best friends and bass players.

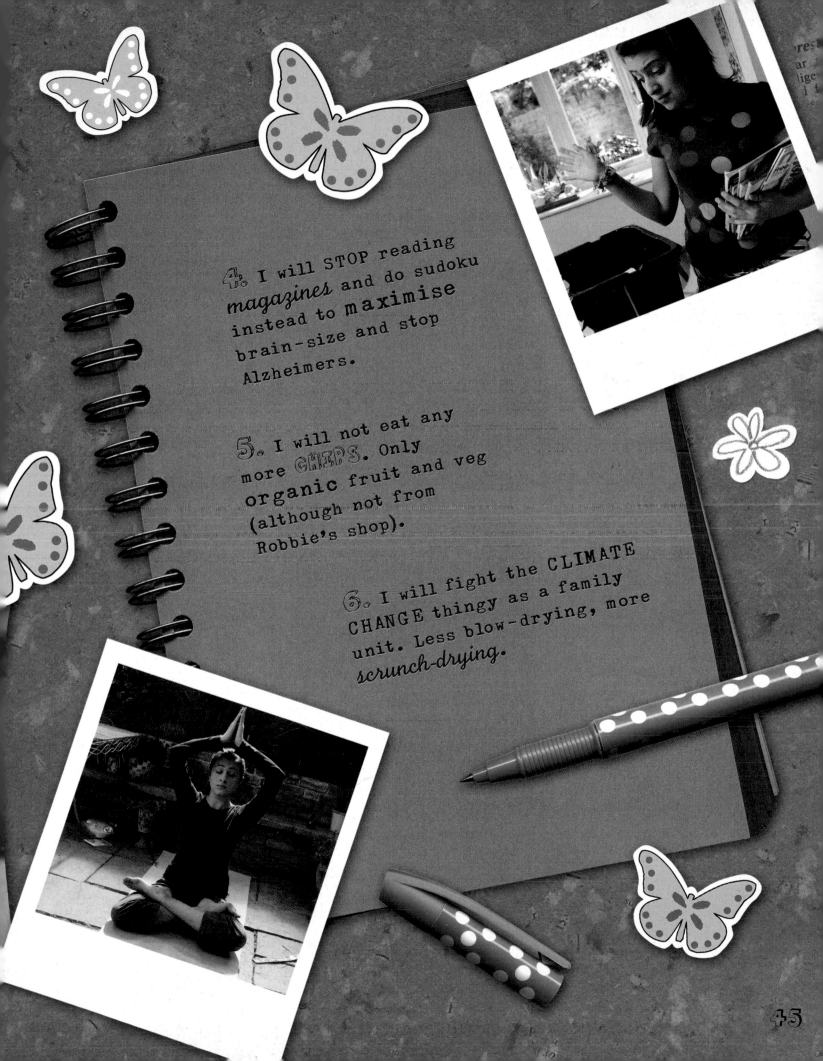

4. I will STOP reading *magazines* and do sudoku instead to **maximise** brain-size and stop Alzheimers.

5. I will not eat any more CHIPS. Only **organic** fruit and veg (although not from Robbie's shop).

6. I will fight the CLIMATE CHANGE thingy as a family unit. Less blow-drying, more *scrunch-drying*.

Beauty School DROP IN

MAKE-UP and *beauty* can turn you from a Pamela Green into a dance floor diva *extraordinaire!*
Here are the top ten TIPS to a perfect look:

1.
Always start with clean, moisturised skin, let your moisturiser sink in for a few minutes before you start with any other make-up, otherwise you'll be Grease City.

2.
Smooth your foundation or tinted moisturiser on to your chin, nose and forehead. Use your fingers to blend it in for a natural finish.

3.
Cover up any blemishes or spots with concealer. Try and have a light touch – the only thing that looks worse than a zit is a zit caked in make-up. Less is more!

4.
Dust loose powder over your whole face to set your foundation and to get rid of any shine. Try not to sneeze!

5.
Use your middle finger to apply a neutral, bronze coloured eyeshadow to your eyelid. Don't go up any higher than the crease or you will start looking like one of those scary women at the bus stop.

6.
Comb some brown/black mascara through your top eyelashes, going slowly to avoid any clumps or lumps.

7.
For your lips,
apply a tinted
gloss or lip balm all
over for a fresh,
natural look.

8.
Using a large,
fluffy brush, dust a
natural blush (pink or
peach) onto the apples of
your cheeks – the roundest
part of your cheeks when you
smile. Or in summer, opt for a
touch of the bronzer, but
don't go wild – you don't
want to be Little Miss
Orange Face.

9.
Dot some
highlighter onto
your cheekbones
and blend in.

10.
Now you're
finished! The most
important beauty tip to
remember is always to
wash your face at the end
of the day. Clogging your
skin up with old
make-up will result
in Zit City.

Now, you've worked out
your basic *make-up*,
here are some top ways
of jazzing up your look.

✪ **Coloured Eye Shadow** Try mixing it up
with some brightly coloured eye shadow.
You can go with gentle shades if you're
nervous and then move onto brighter
colours when you're feeling a bit braver!

✪ **Glitter** This looks great on the tops of your
cheekbones or dotted in the corner of your eyes.
But don't go too overboard – you don't want to
look like you're made out of metal!

✪ **Lipstick** If you love your lippy, try some bolder
colours like deep berry shades, bright red, light pink
and even sparkly, glittery colours.

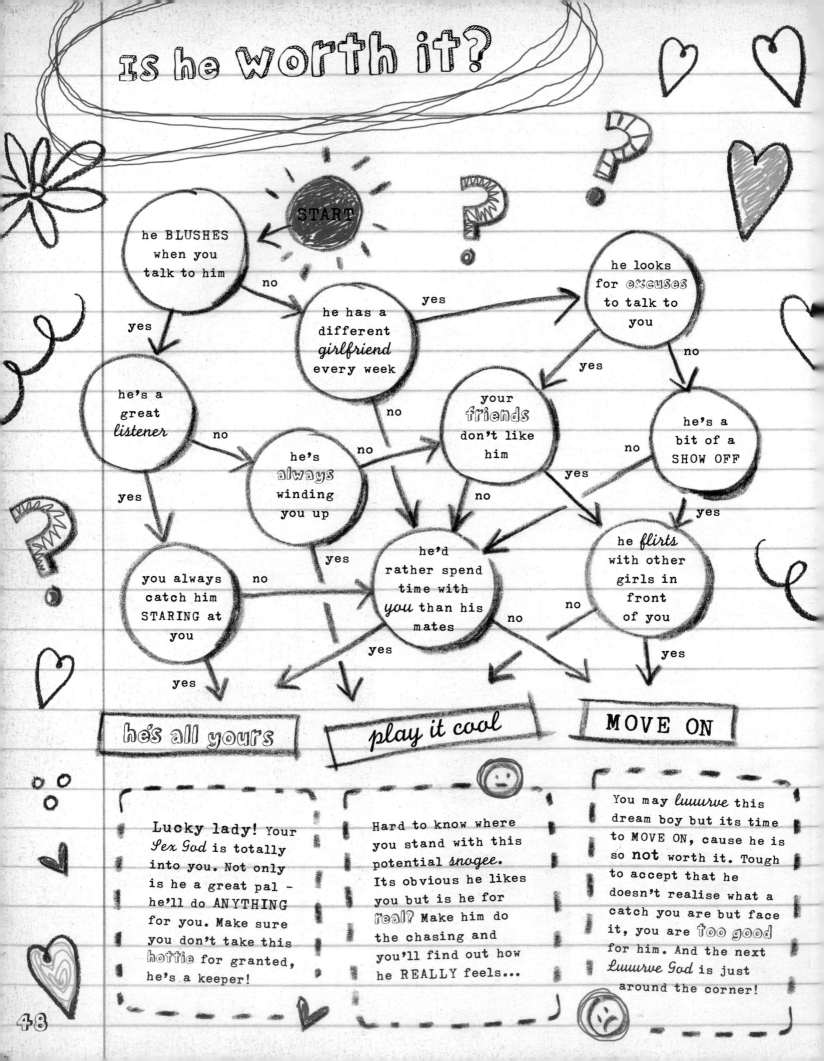

Is he worth it?

START

he BLUSHES when you talk to him
— no → he has a different *girlfriend* every week
— yes → he looks for *excuses* to talk to you

he BLUSHES when you talk to him — yes → he's a great *listener*

he looks for *excuses* to talk to you — no → he's a bit of a SHOW OFF
he looks for *excuses* to talk to you — yes → your *friends* don't like him

he's a great *listener* — no → he's *always* winding you up
he's a great *listener* — yes → you always catch him STARING at you

he's *always* winding you up — no → your *friends* don't like him
he's *always* winding you up — yes → he'd rather spend time with *you* than his mates

your *friends* don't like him — yes → he'd rather spend time with *you* than his mates
your *friends* don't like him — no → he flirts with other girls in front of you

he's a bit of a SHOW OFF — no → he'd rather spend time with *you* than his mates
he's a bit of a SHOW OFF — yes → he flirts with other girls in front of you

you always catch him STARING at you — no → he'd rather spend time with *you* than his mates
you always catch him STARING at you — yes → **he's all yours**

he'd rather spend time with *you* than his mates — yes → **he's all yours**
he'd rather spend time with *you* than his mates — no → he flirts with other girls in front of you

he flirts with other girls in front of you — no → *play it cool*
he flirts with other girls in front of you — yes → **MOVE ON**

he's all yours

Lucky lady! Your *Sex God* is totally into you. Not only is he a great pal – he'll do ANYTHING for you. Make sure you don't take this *hottie* for granted, he's a keeper!

play it cool

Hard to know where you stand with this potential *snogee*. Its obvious he likes you but is he for *real*? Make him do the chasing and you'll find out how he REALLY feels...

MOVE ON

You may *luuurve* this dream boy but its time to MOVE ON, cause he is so **not** worth it. Tough to accept that he doesn't realise what a catch you are but face it, you are *too good* for him. And the next *Luuurve God* is just around the corner!

Georgia goes down to the beach
hoping to see Robbie there...

So she can apologise to him...

...and let him know that she's
moving away.

Which is the worst timing ever,
cause Robbie tells her he's just
dumped Lindsay!

Do-er Quiz

1. What makes eyelashes longer, according to Georgia?

a. Crying
b. Vaseline
c. Mascara

2. Who is the thong wearer (from Vulgaria)?

a. Robbie
b. Lindsay
c. Pamela Green

3. What is Peter Dyer's catchphrase?

a. The man of the snog
b. The man, the myth, the legend
c. The man of mystery

4. What beauty blunder does Georgia make before going swimming?

a. Overdoing it with the Kool-tan
b. Forgetting to shave her legs
c. Applying non-waterproof mascara

5. Who is Georgia's 'red herring'?

a. Tom
b. Robbie
c. Dave the Laugh

6. What does Georgia nag her mum for?

a. A boob job
b. A nose job
c. A face lift

7. What is number five on the snogging scale?

a. Open mouth kissing
b. Holding hands
c. Goodnight kiss

8. Where do the Stiff Dylans play their gig?

a. Brighton
b. Newcastle
c. Leeds

9. From which book does Georgia learn about elastic band theory?

a. Men are from Mars, Women are from Venus
b. Men are from Venus, Women are from Mars
c. Men and Women are Aliens

10. What are the two important 'osities' according to Georgia?

a. Maturiosity and Icicleosity
b. Immaturiosity and Glaciosity
c. Maturiosity and Glaciosity

11. What does Libby do when she meets Robbie?

a. Licks his hand
b. Barks like a dog
c. Burps at him

12. What does Georgia call Eastbourne?

a. Sad City
b. God's Waiting Room
c. Rock City

13. What does Georgia's mum tell Robbie about apples?

a. They're Georgia's favourite fruit
b. They make Georgia throw up
c. They give Georgia wind

14. Which nightclub does Lindsay say she's booked for her party?

a. 5th Avenue
b. Tramps
c. Sheiks

15. According to Robbie, who are the Stiff Dylans musical influences?

a. Jay-Z and The Kooks
b. The Bee Gees and Rhianna
c. Radiohead and Pink Floyd

16. Whose party does Georgia accidentally flash her knickers at?

a. Kirstie Walsh
b. Katie Welsh
c. Kylie Wish

17. Can you name the DJ Lindsay books for her party?

a. Tim Westwood
b. Chris Moyles
c. Fat Boy Slim

18. Who does Georgia's dad book for her party?

a. Paul Daniels
b. Derren Brown
c. Coco the Clown

19. What is Lindsay's secret enhancement?

a. Support tights
b. Hair extensions
c. Chicken fillets (i.e. gel bra inserts)

20. According to Peter Dyer, how many snogs does the average person have in a lifetime?

a. More than 26,000
b. More than a million
c. More than 300

21. What breaks off in Robbie's hand?

a. Georgia's fake nail
b. Georgia's blonde streak
c. Georgia's stiletto heel

22. What eternal conundrum does Tom say to Jas?

a. See you later
b. Call me sometime
c. I'll be around

23. What new song does Robbie write for Georgia?

a. Aquamarine
b. Ultraviolet
c. Hot pink

24. What pet does Robbie own?

a. Cat
b. Dog
c. Rabbit

25. What sports game are the girls playing when Lindsay attacks Georgia?

a. Squash
b. Netball
c. Hockey

26. What does Libby like doing best?

a. Drawing on Georgia's school books
b. Making Angus wear fancy dress
c. Hiding in the fridge

Answers on page 60-61

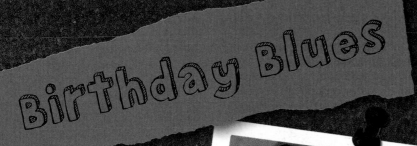

Birthday Blues

After her bust up with Jas, Georgia has cancelled her party (she's sure everyone will be at Lindsay's anyway).

In the morning, Mum and Libby try to cheer her up with cake, a shopping trip and

getting ready for a family night out...

Planning the Perfect... Party Outfit

Choosing the *perfect* party outfit can be trickier than you think. Turning up dressed as a stuffed olive when all your mates are in slinky *babe* outfits will not be your finest moment. Use these handy Q and As to work out what NOT to wear!

1. How are you getting to the party?
a) You're walking
b) Your parents are driving you there (or driving alongside you if you've gone for the stuffed olive outfit)
c) Your friend's parents are collecting everyone

2. What kind of party is it?
a) A sleepover party
b) There's gonna be dancing
c) Don't really know

3. Does the invite say what you should wear?
a) It says to bring PJs
b) It says dress to impress but I'm not sure what that means
c) It doesn't say anything!

4. Where is the party?
a) My friend's house
b) At a club
c) I'm not sure. I think it's at a restaurant but I could be wrong

5. What is your best friend wearing?
a) Just her normal clothes
b) She's got a new dress and heels
c) She asked me!

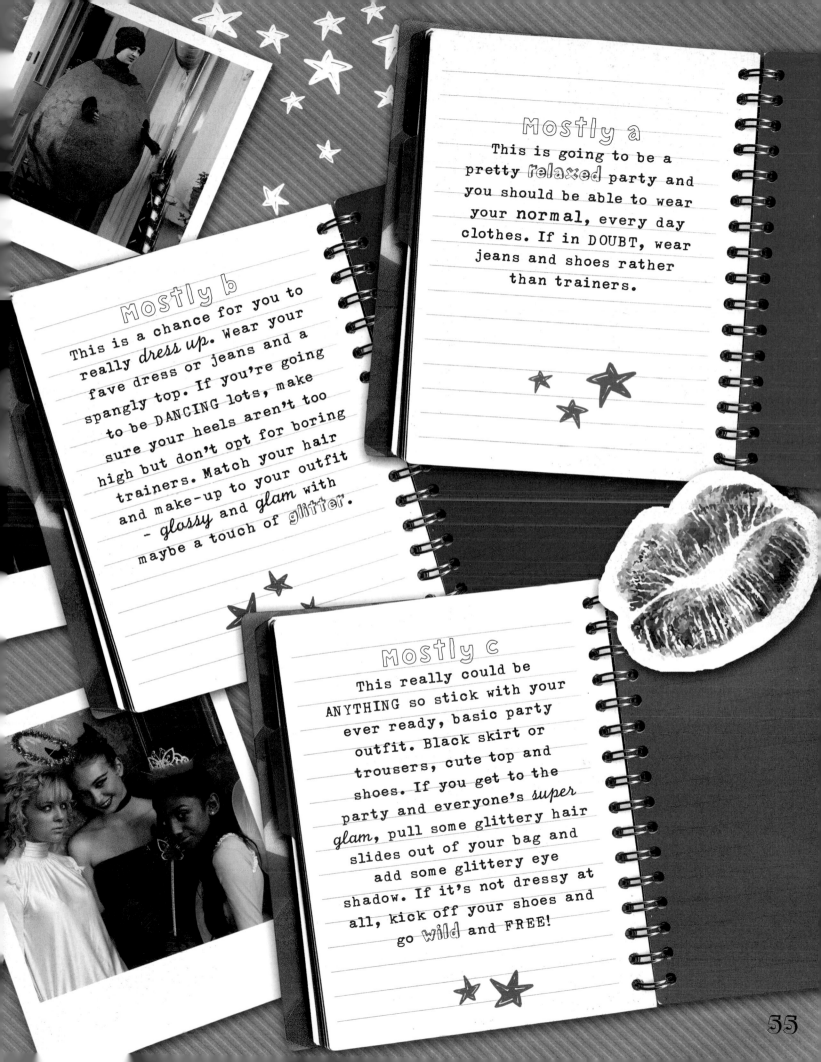

Mostly a

This is going to be a pretty *relaxed* party and you should be able to wear your **normal**, every day clothes. If in DOUBT, wear jeans and shoes rather than trainers.

Mostly b

This is a chance for you to really *dress up*. Wear your fave dress or jeans and a spangly top. If you're going to be DANCING lots, make sure your heels aren't too high but don't opt for boring trainers. Match your hair and make-up to your outfit – *glossy* and *glam* with maybe a touch of *glitter*.

Mostly c

This really could be ANYTHING so stick with your ever ready, basic party outfit. Black skirt or trousers, cute top and shoes. If you get to the party and everyone's *super glam*, pull some glittery hair slides out of your bag and add some glittery eye shadow. If it's not dressy at all, kick off your shoes and go *wild* and FREE!

Georgia RULES!

The worst birthday ever becomes...the best!

Georgia's mum and Jas have pulled out all the stops so Georgia gets the coolest surprise party ever...

All of the Ace Gang are there

And Georgia and Jas are besties again

Dad is back too!

Lindsay's party at Tramps is going less than well

but back at Georgia's, Stiff Dylans are rocking the crowd,

Mum and Dad are reunited

Even grandad's there

and onstage Robbie gives Georgia a perfect snog!

It's time to paaaaaaarty!

We hope you've enjoyed Top Gossip
and now are experts in the marvy world of
Georgia and her fabbity-fab film,
Angus, Thongs and Perfect Snogging.

There's heaps of **new** things for you to go
away and try, from recipes and
themed parties, to outfits and
beauty tips so you can be

Fabbity-fab too!

X

Answers

PAGE 23-24
All About Georgia Quiz

1. a. Libby
2. a. Ridgley
3. c. New Zealand
4. c. A mobile phone
5. b. Slim
6. a. Lindsay Marling
7. a. The Scottish Highlands
8. c. Robbie
9. b. Stuffed olive
10. a. Peter Dyer
11. a. Jas, Rosie, Ellen and Georgia
12. b. Her nose
13. a. Jas
14. b. Connie
15. c. Bob
16. c. Kiwi-land
17. b. Mexican restaurant

PAGE 29-31
Ace Gang Quiz

1. c. Sweden
2. c. Tom
3. c. An attack of the nerves
4. b. Sven
5. c. Stiff Dylans
6. a. Stand-up comedian
7. c. Helping out at his mum's organic shop
8. b. London
9. c. Hamsters
10. b. Jem
11. c. Salsa dancing
12. a. Lulu
13. c. Shaves off one of her eyebrows
14. a. Bass guitar
15. c. The Bummer Twins
16. b. The Angus Advantage
17. a. P.E. teacher

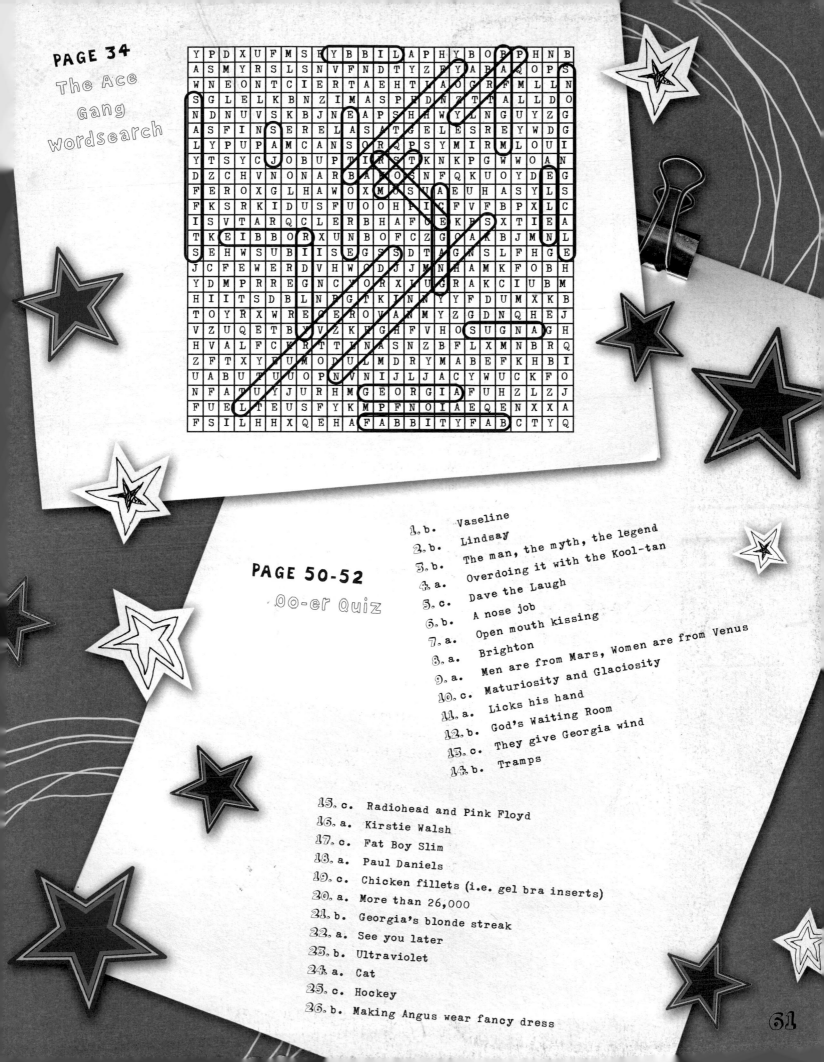

PAGE 50-52

Oo-er Quiz

1. b. Vaseline
2. b. Lindsay
3. b. The man, the myth, the legend
4. a. Overdoing it with the Kool-tan
5. c. Dave the Laugh
6. b. A nose job
7. a. Open mouth kissing
8. a. Brighton
9. a. Men are from Mars, Women are from Venus
10. c. Maturiosity and Glaciosity
11. a. Licks his hand
12. b. God's Waiting Room
13. c. They give Georgia wind
14. b. Tramps

15. c. Radiohead and Pink Floyd
16. a. Kirstie Walsh
17. c. Fat Boy Slim
18. a. Paul Daniels
19. c. Chicken fillets (i.e. gel bra inserts)
20. a. More than 26,000
21. b. Georgia's blonde streak
22. a. See you later
23. b. Ultraviolet
24. a. Cat
25. c. Hockey
26. b. Making Angus wear fancy dress

Now read the *fabbity-fab*
Confessions of Georgia Nicolson
by patron saint of Scottish Wildcats and
number ONE author, Louise Rennison.

NUMBER ONE BESTSELLING AUTHOR

Angus,
thongs
and
full-
frontal
snogging

You'll laugh
your knickers off!

Louise Rennison

ISBN: 978-0-00-721867-7

NUMBER ONE BESTSELLING AUTHOR

'It's
OK, I'm
wearing
really
big
knickers!'

Fabulously funny!

Louise Rennison

ISBN: 978-0-00-721868-4

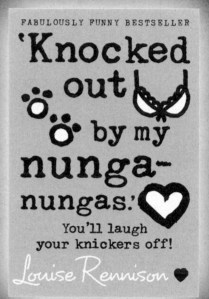

FABULOUSLY FUNNY BESTSELLER

'Knocked
out
by my
nunga-
nungas.'

You'll laugh
your knickers off!

Louise Rennison

ISBN: 978-0 0-00-721869-1

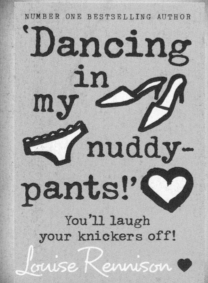

NUMBER ONE BESTSELLING AUTHOR

'Dancing
in
my
nuddy-
pants!'

You'll laugh
your knickers off!

Louise Rennison

ISBN: 978-0-00-721870-7

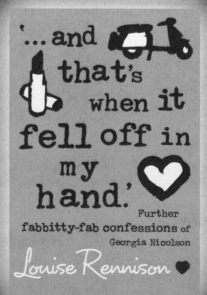

'...and
that's
when it
fell off in
my
hand.'
Further
fabbitty-fab confessions of
Georgia Nicolson

Louise Rennison

ISBN: 978-0-00-718320-3

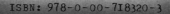

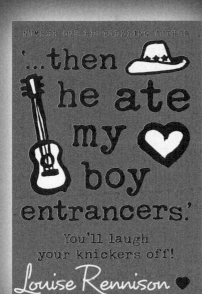

'…then he ate my ♥ boy entrancers.'

You'll laugh your knickers off!

Louise Rennison ♥

ISBN: 978-0-00-718321-0

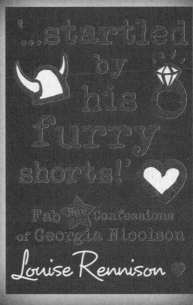

'…startled by his furry shorts!'

Fab New Confessions of Georgia Nicolson

Louise Rennison ♥

ISBN: 978-0-00-722209-4

'Luuurve is a ♪ many trousered thing…'

Fab New Confessions of Georgia Nicolson

Louise Rennison ♥

ISBN: 978-0-00-722211-7

Coming soon:

'Stop in the ♥ name of pants!'

Fab New Confessions of Georgia Nicolson

Louise Rennison ♥

ISBN: 978-0-00-727583-0

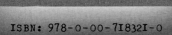